Why is the Cow on the Roof?

Books by the same author

Idle Jack
Smart Girls
Smart Girls Forever

Robert Leeson

Why is the Cow on the Roof?

illustrated by
Axel Scheffler

WALKER BOOKS

First published 1998 by Walker Books Ltd
87 Vauxhall Walk, London SE11 5HJ

This edition published 2017

2 4 6 8 10 9 7 5 3 1

Text © 1998 Robert Leeson
Illustrations © 1998, 2017 Axel Scheffler

This book has been typeset in Plantin

Printed and bound by CPI Group (UK) Ltd, Croydon CR0 4YY

British Library Cataloguing in Publication Data:
a catalogue record for this book is available from the British Library

ISBN 978-1-4063-8053-8

www.walker.co.uk

Contents

Why is the Cow on the Roof?

Why is the Cow on the Roof?

Ola and Kari made a splendid couple, that's what everyone said. He was tall and broad-shouldered and hard working, she was quick and cheerful.

They lived in a cottage right up against the mountain, with their little baby, who crawled around the kitchen floor and gurgled and put things in its mouth to see what they tasted like.

In the shed outside lived a brown cow who supplied them with milk and cream, and behind the shed lived a black-and-white pig who was going to supply them with pork chops and bacon, but the pig didn't know that yet.

Every day Ola kissed Kari, took up his scythe and marched off to work in the fields while she got busy round the house.

And when the sun was well over the mountain-top, Kari would walk up the valley and call Ola to come down and have his dinner. So it went on day after day. It couldn't be better. In fact, they ought to have lived happily ever after.

But there was just one thing wrong.

Now and then, Kari was a little late calling Ola for his dinner. He'd come down to the cottage and find her sitting by the fire talking to the baby while she stirred the porridge in the pot.

"There you are, Ola," she would say. "Is that the time already? I've been so busy I forgot to come and call you."

Ola answered grumpily, "Busy doing what? I've moved halfway down Ten Acre Meadow and you've just been sitting here watching the pot and playing with the baby. I'd love a job like that."

Kari smiled at him. "Oh, Ola, you have no idea how many things there are to do in the house. There's butter to churn for our dinner, the cow to feed and water, the kitchen to clean, the porridge to boil. And all the time I've got to watch the baby – and as for that pig, you need an eye on each finger to keep up with him."

"All that, eh?" said Ola. "And what do you do for the rest of the day? Read a book?"

Kari shook her head. "You don't know. The time goes – if it's not one thing, it's another. I hardly have a minute to turn round."

Ola was tired and grumpy and wouldn't be talked into a good mood. "Huh. I could do all that in half an hour, with one hand tied behind my back."

"Could you now?" Kari was beginning to get a little annoyed. But she changed her tone and put her arm around her husband's shoulder. "Look, let's not quarrel over who does most work. Let's find out."

Ola was suspicious. "What does that mean?"

"Tomorrow we'll swap places. What d'you

say? I'll go off haymaking and you stay home and look after the house. That way we'll see who works hardest."

"Why not?" Ola cheered up right away. "I like the idea." While he talked he was looking round the kitchen and working out how he would run the show, ha ha, and not have to slog up to Ten Acre Meadow and cut hay all day.

So they both went to bed in a good mood.

Early next morning Kari took the scythe over her shoulder and set off up the valley to join the haymakers. Ola waved her goodbye with a grin on his face and then got busy round the kitchen. Well begun is half done, everyone knows that. He'd soon have it sorted.

First he checked the baby was safe in the corner playing with its toys. Then he got cream from the dairy, poured it into the churn and began to swing the handle to turn it into butter.

After five minutes' hard churning he began

to sweat. Take it easy, Ola, he told himself.
No hurry. He opened the churn, but the
butter wasn't set. So he started to churn
again, a little more slowly.

By the time the butter was nearly ready, so
was he – for some light refreshment.
Everything was going well – this job was a
doddle. So he nipped down into the cellar for
a drink of beer.

There was just one snag. The barrel hadn't
been tapped. He looked round. Now which
idiot had moved the mallet? Then he
remembered. He'd used it yesterday and left
it in the kitchen. Up the steps, quick look to
see baby was happy, and then down into the
cellar again. With a couple of sharp blows he
knocked out the bung. Now he just had to fit
the spigot into the hole and he could tap off a
nice cool pint.

But as he stood with the spigot in one hand
and the mallet in the other, he heard a
strange scraping noise overhead. It didn't
take him long to figure it out. The pig had

sneaked into the kitchen.

He was halfway up the ladder when there was an almighty crash. He knew in a flash what it was – the pig had knocked over the churn! He was right. As he burst into the kitchen, cream and butter were running over the floor and the pig was lapping it up.

"You greedy swine!" yelled Ola and leapt across the room. The pig headed for the door, but not quickly enough. Rage gave Ola extra speed. He caught the black-and-white thief on the threshold and with one mighty kick stretched it out on the ground.

It didn't move. Ola looked down at it in dismay. Then he shrugged. They were going to kill it later in the year anyway. First things first. Back to churning butter – for, being smart, he had left some cream in the dairy. He set to work again.

Then he stopped. Why was he standing here with the mallet in one hand and the spigot in the other? The beer barrel! Like a shot he was down in the cellar. But too late – the barrel had run dry. The kitchen floor ran with cream, the cellar floor with beer.

Back upstairs went Ola to churn more butter. He'd have to wait a while for his drink. Still there were always teething problems.

But, someone else was thirsty. From the shed came a mournful moo. He'd forgotten to give the brown cow her water and let her out in the orchard to graze.

This needed quick thinking. If he went out to the shed, there'd be no trouble with the pig, who wasn't going anywhere. But the baby was crawling around and might tug on the churn and topple it over.

Well, Ola was more than a match for this problem. He slung the churn over his shoulder, got the bucket and went across the yard to the little stream that flowed nearby to get water for the cow.

However, as he bent down to fill the pail, the lid fell off the churn and the half-churned cream ran down over his neck.

Was he discouraged? Not he! He filled the bucket, went back to the shed, let the cow out and gave her a long drink. She thanked him very much for that.

Now it was clear to a sharp chap like Ola that he couldn't take the cow down to the orchard and leave the baby alone. But he had the answer. The cottage was roofed with turf and in the summer the turf grew grass like a little field. In two shakes he had the cow up the slope behind the cottage, and he'd bridged the gap between this and the roof with a plank. With a little urging he persuaded the cow to walk along it, and soon she was happily grazing on the roof. Down went Ola to the kitchen again.

But quick as he was, time was passing quickly too. He had to get the porridge going. So he filled the pot with water and hung it over the fire. And while he was pouring in the oats, a thought struck him.

What if the cow should slip off the roof?

If that happened all his livestock would be deadstock. He didn't hang about, but took a rope and climbed swiftly onto the roof. It was a moment's work to tie one end of the rope round the cow's neck and pass the other end down the chimney.

Back in the kitchen, he took the rope end dangling down the chimney and tied it round his own leg, keeping both arms free. All was going well now. The cow was grazing on the roof, the baby was gurgling in the corner, the pig was lying – very quietly – outside the kitchen door and the porridge was in the pot. Ah, but now he needed the ladle to stir it with.

He stared across the kitchen to the row of hooks where the ladles hung. As he moved, the cow was pulled by the rope right up against the chimney. She didn't care for that and nor would you. So she pulled back just as Ola was taking down the ladle, and he was drawn across the kitchen floor towards the fireplace.

Not to be pushed around – or pulled – by a cow, Ola jerked back and set off across the room again. Up on the roof the cow braced herself and heaved in the opposite direction. To and fro they went in a mad tug of war.

But weight and four legs count. Ola's feet went from under him. The cow slipped backwards, staggered and fell off the roof, while Ola slid faster and faster until he shot, feet first, up the chimney. She hung down outside while he hung down inside.

Now, about the time that Ola had set the porridge to boil in the pot, Kari finished mowing Ten Acre Meadow. The sun had climbed right across the sky. When was Ola coming to call her home to dinner? There was no sign of him, so she put the scythe over her shoulder and set off down the valley. Soon enough she came in sight of the cottage.

She stopped in amazement. She could not believe her eyes. What on earth was the cow doing, waltzing around the roof like that? And just as she asked the question the cow *fell off* and hung at the end of her tether, swinging a few feet from the ground.

She'll choke herself, thought Kari. Running across the yard she gave one quick swipe of the scythe blade, cut the rope and the cow dropped safely down to earth.

Next Kari caught sight of the pig lying in the doorway. What was going on? As she hurried up, the pig opened one eye and looked at her – but couldn't answer her question.

Neither could the baby, who was happily playing in the middle of a pool of cream on the kitchen floor.

And neither could Ola, who was standing on his head in the porridge.

Are You Calling Me a Liar, Sire?

Are You Calling Me a Liar, Sire?

King Boris was a mighty monarch, a renowned ruler, a celebrated sovereign. His kingdom stretched from here right over to there, and further still, if the kingdom next door didn't mind being invaded. And even if it did, it kept very quiet, for Boris was a king of tremendous temper and horrendous habits.

And his worst habit was – enjoying himself.

On a summer Sunday evening, there was nothing he liked better than to sit on his throne and listen to stories. Storytellers would come from miles around to entertain the court – to amaze the mighty monarch and his proud dukes and duchesses, his holy bishops and the plump, wealthy merchants.

They came in hopes of a rich reward. Beside the king's throne stood a great, open oak chest full to the brim with gleaming gold coins, glowing rubies, flashing diamonds and amethysts blue as the evening sky. This was the prize which awaited the person who could tell such a fantastical tale that the king would refuse to believe it.

At first the minstrels of the kingdom, and realms beyond the sea, beat a path to King Boris's door. But as the weeks passed and each Sunday evening came around, the queue of storytellers grew smaller and smaller and smaller.

The truth was, there was a snag to the king's entertainment.

On the other side of the throne stood a second oak chest, with the lid thrown back. And in that chest was an enormous two-edged shining sword. Any storyteller whose tale failed to make the king roar "You're a liar!" had his head whipped off.

And King Boris had seen so much in his long and lusty life that it was impossible to shock or even surprise him.

So it came about that one Sunday evening

the courtiers, the proud dukes and duchesses, the holy bishops and the plump, wealthy merchants stood in fear and trembling. There was no one waiting at the entrance to the royal hall, ready to step forward and tell the tale.

A deathly hush fell over the court as King Boris took his place on the throne and looked around him. "Well, well," he rumbled, "what a disappointment – no storyteller tonight. I don't know. I can remember the time when minstrels and all sorts would be fighting for the chance to win the treasure chest. I can't think what's come over people. Can you?"

"No, Your Majesty," they answered, as one man, or woman.

"Well," said the king, "there's only one thing for it. One of you will have to stand in for tonight. If we can't have a professional, we'll make do with an amateur. Who's it going to be? Usual rules, usual reward. Come on, let's get started."

But not a single voice answered.

"Oh, dear!" boomed the king. "I hate to do this, but we shall have to pick names out of a hat." He looked round. "What a po-faced bunch you are, to be sure. No imagination, no spirit of adventure. Lord Chancellor!"

"Yes, Sire?" quavered the official, who was usually very grand and haughty.

"Where's your hat?"

"I – I left it at home, Your Majesty."

King Boris's face began to turn a violety purple, not like an amethyst, more like a thundercloud.

"Very well, then. *I'll* choose someone."

There was a ripple of sound throughout the throne room as noble knees began to knock together, when suddenly a herald at the door called out, "S-s-ire! I think I see a st-story-teller coming over the courtyard."

Everyone hurried to the windows to look out. Then, despite their fears, they all began to point and laugh.

Ambling across the great square in front of

the palace door was a broken-down old mule. But the mule looked in better shape than the rider, who was dressed in a ragged shirt and trousers. As he dismounted and bent to tie up his mount, the trousers split across and the shirt popped out.

A moment later that stranger entered the throne room and took from his head an old hat with a feather two feet long. He marched so grandly that everyone made way for him.

"All right then," said he, "where's this king who wants to hear a story?"

No one answered. King Boris, sitting there plain to see on his throne, did not know whether to laugh or be furious at this impertinence. But in a voice that shook the chandeliers he bellowed, "I'm here!"

The stranger did not bat an eyelid, but answered, "Oh, yes. Well, you're togged up like a king, but what does that prove? Anyone can get themselves up in fancy dress. I mean, look at me. When I'm in my

Sunday best, you wouldn't guess that I'm practically skint, now would you?"

The courtiers started to titter, but King Boris silenced them with a glance. "That's true," he told the new arrival. "An elegant outfit like yours makes a world of difference. Might I know who you are and which great estate you own?"

"My name's Michael Muck," came the answer, "and once the land I owned was so wide that a calf born on one side of my property would be a full grown bull before it grazed its way to the other."

Everyone held their breath at this amazing claim. But King Boris simply said, "I believe you. And did you have many cattle?"

"Millions," said ragged Michael. "So many that when we wanted to make cheese we had to drain the largest lake and fill it with milk. One day a foal dropped into the lake and we found it in the middle of the cheese five years later – a full grown horse."

The courtiers started to snigger again. But

King Boris smiled craftily. "And how did it happen that you lost this vast estate?"

Michael nodded to the crowd behind him. "Oh, the merchants, greedy gutsers every one of them, took it off me."

"You rogue!" called out the merchants. "We never did. When did all this happen?"

"Don't you remember?" asked Michael. "In the year of the Great Famine."

"What Great Famine?" they protested.

"Don't you remember?" asked Michael. "All the poor folk were starving and selling their land to you scoundrels."

"They never were," chorused the merchants.

"Are you calling me a liar?" challenged the ragged man. That shut them up and made King Boris chuckle and say, "I believe you. These merchants would swindle their own mothers."

He waved to Michael. "Go on, tell me. How did you survive the Great Famine?"

"Nothing simpler, Sire," went on Michael.

"I went to Australia, where they had masses of cheap corn."

"And how did you cross the great ocean?"

"Nothing easier. I jumped over. It was a leap year, you see. Then once I'd reached Australia, the Emperor asked me how much corn I needed. So I said, 'Now, let's take this chessboard with sixty-four squares. I'll have one grain on the first square, two on the second, four on the third and eight on the fourth. Just keep doubling the number.'

"'Easy peasy,' said the Emperor of Australia. But he changed his tune because by the time the board was full, every grain of corn had gone from his granaries."

King Boris smiled. "Serves him right. But how did you get the corn back over the ocean?"

"Would you believe," laughed Michael, "I tipped it all into the sea, and the water was so hot it turned into porridge. Folk on the farther side just brought their bowls and helped themselves."

"Very ingenious," nodded the king. "And

what happened then?"

Michael continued. "I had only two acres of land left. One day I was out ploughing with the old grey mare when her back broke in two. So I joined it up with twigs from a willow tree and she was twice as good as before. But, you know, the willow twigs started to grow. They grew right up into the sky. And just for a lark I climbed up the tree into Heaven."

"Outrageous!" spluttered the Bishops.

Michael shook his head. "Not at all. It was Sunday evening and God and the archangels were at home playing cards. They asked me to take a hand."

"That can't be true!" How shocked the Bishops sounded!

"Are you calling me a liar?" demanded Michael.

"Of course they're not!" roared the king. "They all play cards on Sunday evening. Go on, Michael lad. Why didn't you stay there – up in Heaven?"

"Alas, the willow tree died. I was worried about the old grey mare. So I spun a rope out of clouds and shinned down it. But, halfway down, the rope ran out. So I reached up to Heaven and pulled down the length I'd climbed down already and let it drop beneath me. But even then it wasn't long enough. So, I let go and fell."

"You fell?" asked the king. "And you're here to tell the tale?"

"If I'm not a liar," answered Michael, "you see me here before you."

"But how on earth...?"

"No problem. I fell through the hole at the top of Mount Etna – and tumbled straight into Hell."

A cry of astonishment went up from the Court but King Boris silenced them with a scowl.

"And were you burnt to death, eh?"

"Not in the least. It was so cold I nearly froze."

"But," the king wrinkled his brow, "I

thought they had a huge fire burning in Hell."

"True enough, Your Majesty, but I couldn't get near it for all the Dukes and Duchesses."

"That's not true!" cried the nobility with one voice.

Michael looked round at them. "Are you calling me a liar, then?"

"Of course they're not," growled the king. "I'm sure every word you've said is true. So, Michael, how did you get out of Hell?"

"I twisted myself round and round like a drill and bored my way into a cave, where there were forty thieves counting their ill-gotten gains. I said to the leader, 'Your face looks familiar.'

"'No wonder,' said he. 'I'm King Boris's father, but these days he doesn't want to know me.'"

The king leapt up from his throne like a jack-in-the-box.

"That's not true, you rogue, Michael Muck!" he cried.

The ragged man smiled triumphantly. "Are you calling me a liar, Sire?"

King Boris turned purple with fury.

"Take the cursed treasure and get out of here!" he roared.

Who's Next
for the Chop?

Who's Next for the Chop?

One evening, a Tailor and his Wife wandered through the city, looking at the shops and listening to the clowns and musicians who performed round the crowded squares.

They bought meat, fish, fruit and sweets for a treat and were just on their way home when they heard someone shouting. A little man was cracking jokes and turning somersaults so comical he had the crowds in stitches with laughter.

"My master asked me," he chortled, "'How many fools are there in this city?' I told him, 'You ought to know. Ask me something sensible like 'How many wise men are there? Apart from myself, I can't think of one.' But did he thank me for my answer? No, he had me beaten and thrown out in the street. So now I'm busking for a living."

While the crowd laughed, the Tailor's Wife said to her husband, "Let's ask the Jester to have supper with us. That'll round off the evening."

So they did, and the three went home and feasted together. The Jester ate and drank and told jokes until he was quite full. When the Tailor's Wife offered him the last morsel on the last plate he refused. "No, I couldn't, Lady. I'm bursting."

"Come on," she urged, "force yourself." And for a joke she took the little man by the chin and popped the fish bit into his mouth. Then a terrible thing happened. First his face went red, then he made choking noises and finally he fell flat and lay still.

"What have you done?" cried the husband, trying to lift up the Jester. "You have killed him. Oh, oh, I shall lose my head for this."

"Fool," snapped his wife. "You've lost your head already."

She ran to fetch a blanket and rolled the little man in it. It was easy, for he was no bigger than a boy.

"Now," she told her husband, "pick him up and come along. Don't say a word. Leave the talking to me."

Rigid with fear, the husband did as he was told. Outside in the crowded street his wife went ahead calling, "Make way, please. Our child is ill with fever, maybe the plague. We must find a doctor."

Like magic the crowd let them through. So they came to the house of the Jewish Doctor. There the wife woke the servant at the outer door and gave him ten dinars to call his master. Once the servant had gone upstairs she said to her husband, "Place the body on the stairs." Which he did.

"Now, let's go quickly." Which they did.

Meanwhile the good Doctor, half asleep, hurrying down, fell over the body of the Jester and sent it hurtling to the foot of the stairs, where it lay still.

"My life!" he cried. "I have killed my patient! Already I am a dead man."

But he did not panic. Instead he picked up the small body and carried it onto the flat roof of his house. Below lay the backyard of his neighbour, Steward at the Palace. The yard was full of bags and barrels.

Carefully the Doctor lowered the Jester in his blanket till he was propped up against the Steward's wall. Having done that he went to bed and fell asleep.

When the Steward got home the moon had risen. By its light he saw the figure of a man in the yard crouching as if to pounce. No coward, the Steward said grimly to himself, "Aha, a thief." Raising the stick he used to make the royal servants move faster, he gave the intruder a shrewd blow, which laid him flat on the ground.

A moment later the Steward realized there was no movement in the body.

"Heaven help me," he moaned, "I meant to thrash the rogue but I have killed him. The Sultan will have my head."

But no fool he, the Steward soon calmed

down. He went to the gate and looked out. The alley behind his house was empty. Bearing the Jester on his shoulder he stole through the back streets until he found a dark corner. There he leaned the body against a wall, where it looked for all the world like a party-goer trying to sober up.

That done the Steward went home. Soon, like the Jewish Doctor and the Tailor and his Wife, he was fast asleep.

Meanwhile, a Wine Merchant, a Christian, was on his way home after a merry supper. As he turned into the lane at the rear of his house he stopped. The moon cast a warning shadow. Thinking he was about to be mugged, he decided quickly – attack is the best defence.

Boldly he sprang and gave the would-be robber a blow on the head. "Take that, you scoundrel!" he shouted.

There was no answer. Without a return blow or even saying goodbye, the other collapsed and lay motionless on the ground.

"What have I done?" said the Wine Merchant. "I have killed him."

And he was doubly unlucky. At that moment, two policemen appeared, seized him and marched him to the house of the Wali, or law and order officer. As the three of them – or four, if you include the Jester – moved along the main street, a crowd of idlers, revellers and market sweepers followed, shouting, "Murder! Justice!"

The noise woke the Wali, who came down. With one look at the body and its killer he said, "This is too high a matter for me. This is a case for the Kadi, the City Magistrate."

"Why, sir?" demanded the first policeman.

"Because the dead man is a Muslim. The other one is a Christian."

At once, the bystanders set up a great howl. "Evil! A Christian has murdered a Muslim!"

By the time the crowd, growing bigger by the minute, reached the Kadi's house, it was nearly dawn. The Kadi was already at his prayers. But he came out into the street.

When he heard what he heard and saw what he saw, he said, sadly, to the Christian Wine Merchant, "Self-defence or not, say your prayers. The dead man is none other than the Sultan's Jester."

So saying, he led the way to the Palace courtyard, followed by the policemen carrying the body, the trembling Wine Merchant and a noisier and noisier crowd. And one by one, the Steward, the Jewish Doctor and the Tailor and his Wife were woken by the clamour. They climbed from their beds and joined the throng.

They did so out of curiosity. But as the crowd neared the Palace they soon began to understand what had happened. Wisely, they kept quiet.

By dawn the Sultan's courtyard was crammed with people. Only four had any idea what was really going on, but everyone knew who was guilty. *"Justice!"* they bellowed.

The din brought the Sultan out onto his

balcony. At once the crowd was silent. "Who demands justice?" asked His Majesty, and the policemen told their story.

Now in the Sultan's city, justice was speedy. The Executioner was called with his assistants and in a trice they had set up the block and sharpened the sword.

At a sign from the Sultan the Wine Merchant said his prayer and knelt down with neck bared. But even as the sword was raised, someone called from the crowd.

"Your Majesty. I beg you. Wait!"

Amazed, the Sultan looked down as the Steward stepped from the crowd, saying, "Lord and Master. Do not add the death of a Christian to that of a Muslim. The Wine Merchant could not have killed the Jester."

"Why not?"

"Because it was I who killed him."

A great cry of astonishment rose from the crowd. As it died down, the Steward told his tale. The Sultan nodded.

"Well done. You are an honest man. But I

fear you must die."

He gave the sign and now the Steward's head was on the block instead of the Wine Merchant's. Once more the Executioner's blade flashed in the sun...

But, did not fall. Another voice from the crowd called a halt. It was the Jewish Doctor.

"Majesty, live for ever. A Muslim must not die for the crime a Jew has committed."

This time the crowd was silent in expectation of more wonders. The Sultan heard out the Jewish Doctor and gave fresh orders. The Executioner was clearly not pleased – he much preferred chopping to changing – but he dare say nothing and simply bared the Doctor's neck for the sword.

Still the deed was not done. Another voice cried out from the crowd. It was the Tailor, who told his story. Shaking his head in bewilderment, the Sultan raised his hand once more.

In vain. The Tailor's Wife rushed forward. "Prince of Justice, hear my plea. The crime was mine from the beginning." Bewildered but silent the Sultan and his subjects heard her out.

"It grieves me," said the Sultan at last, "but if your story is true, then justice demands..."

This time, the Executioner's patience was exhausted.

"Majesty. When is this farce to end? I am a craftsman. How can I do my work? How do we know there aren't a thousand in this crowd who all want their head seeing to?"

The crowd roared, but with laughter this time. The Sultan bade them be quiet and said, "Let all five stand forward." When they had, he continued.

"Kadi. You must rule. Three Muslims, a Christian and a Jew all claim to have killed the Jester. Who is guilty?"

The Kadi stroked his beard. "If we cannot say which blow actually ended his life, then it may be all are innocent."

"No!" bellowed the crowd.

"On the other hand, it could be that all are guilty."

"Hurrah!" roared the crowd. The Sultan raised his hand and all were still, awaiting his decision.

But in the silence, someone else spoke. "On the other hand, the Kadi may not know what he is talking about."

"Who said that?"

A tall man in white stepped forward. "I, Sire. I am a Barber, and also a Surgeon. The Kadi knows about religion. But I know the difference between life and death…"

"And…?" said the Sultan grimly.

"The Jester is not dead!"

"Not dead?" The crowd spoke as one.

"If Your Majesty permits…" The Barber bent over the Jester's body. A moment later he held up a large fish bone. In that instant the Jester sprang up and cried out as if nothing had happened.

"…So I said to my master – only a fool would ask a question like that."

For a moment the Sultan looked furious. Then he began to chuckle as he remembered why he had caused the Jester to be beaten and driven out. At once the crowd joined in the laughter.

The Sultan rewarded the Barber handsomely. He paid the Executioner double time. He compensated the Tailor, his Wife, the Doctor, the Steward and the Wine Merchant.

"And me, Master!" called out the Jester. "What shall be my reward?"

"You," retorted the Sultan, "shall have your job back and be excused the second beating you richly deserve."

"Ah, Master, you are smarter than I thought," replied the Jester.

At which the crowd laughed again and went home in good spirits.

Why Are You Such a Noddy, Big Ears?

Why Are You Such a Noddy, Big Ears?

Long, long ago, when the Earth was freshly made out of mud and water, everything and everybody was very different from today. Rabbit, for example, walked on two legs like a man, had a fine straight nose, short ears and a long bushy tail, and he hunted with a bow and arrow. But he wasn't very clever and he wasn't very brave.

He thought to himself, everyone's smarter and bolder than me. If I do what they do, things can only get better. So he kept his eye on what other people were doing.

One day as he tracked through the woods, he heard someone singing: *"Oh, today I feel so happy, so happy, so happy."*

Looking up Rabbit saw, at the top of a pine tree, a man caught in the cleft of a split branch.

"Why are you so happy, brother?" asked Rabbit.

"Because up here I can see for miles. I can spot all the game – buffalo, deer, you name it."

"That must be great," said Rabbit. He thought about it for a while, then went on, "Would you change places?"

"What, lose my lookout post and miss out on all the best hunting? Think again."

"If I let you have a go with my bow and arrow?" offered Rabbit.

"Now you're talking," said the man in the tree.

So Rabbit climbed up, put his foot in the cleft of the branch and released the hunter. Cheerfully, the man took Rabbit's bow and arrow, climbed down the tree and ran away.

Rabbit called after him, "Brother, just one question: How do I get down when I've found the game? And what do I hunt with?"

The man laughed. "Just wait until some other fool comes along and ask him."

Well, Rabbit waited and waited. But no one came. Days passed. He was so hungry his stomach rubbed on his backbone. In the end, he grew so thin he pulled himself out and went home.

But by this time everyone had heard about his adventure and they would pull his leg, asking, "Keeping a good lookout, eh, Brother Rabbit?"

With no bow and arrow, Rabbit could not hunt and so he was often hungry. He began to look round for the right wood to make a new set. He wandered far from his home patch until one day he saw a little hut. It had a single window and a man was looking out.

"Hello," said Rabbit. "How are you?"

"I'm fine," came the answer. "Life could not be better. No work. Three square meals a day, and a bed. A good view. What more do I need?"

"I could use a deal like that," said Rabbit.

"Then why don't we swap places?" asked the man.

"Are you sure?" Rabbit was a little surprised by this generosity.

"Well, to tell you the truth," explained the man, "I get a little bored in here sometimes. Does that sort of thing bother you?"

"Not a bit," Rabbit told him. So he took the bar off the door and let the man out. Rabbit went in, lay down on the bed and waited for his supper.

In the evening people from the nearby village came and looked in. "What are you doing here, Rabbit?" they asked in amazement.

"Waiting for my next meal," said he.

"You noddy! This is our jail! The man you let out has been put away. He's on bread and water."

They didn't know whether to be angry or to laugh at Rabbit. But back in his own village, everyone thought he was truly ridiculous. So in the end, Rabbit became despondent.

"What am I?" he brooded. "No one's

afraid of me. They all despise me. I might as well jump in the river."

And with that, he ran down the slope to the river's edge. But he made such a noise that all the frogs basking on the bank jumped up in alarm and leapt into the water.

"Ho ho," laughed Rabbit. "So there *is* someone left in the world who's afraid of me. I think I'll live after all."

Not only did Rabbit live, but he became something of a hero. This is how it happened.

One year the winter was terribly hard. There had never been so much snow and ice. The wind was like a knife. No one could go out and hunt, not even gather wood. In the village the fires went out one by one. Darkness and starvation threatened the Earth people. They were at their wits' end.

There were fires still burning in the world, but they were high on the mountain peaks where the magic Sky People lived, close to the Sun. Their flames never died. But they would not share them with the Earth People. "No," they said, "you let your fires go out, now you must pay for your carelessness."

The Earth People could not live without fire. There was only one way out. They would have to steal fire from the Sky People. But who would do it? Who was brave or crazy enough to take the risk?

At last they made up their minds. "Let's ask Rabbit. He's foolish enough not to know the danger. And if they catch him he won't be missed." So they did.

Rabbit was flattered. No one had ever asked for his help. He put on a big headdress like the ones the Sky People wore and stole up the hill to where they danced around their blazing fire. No one bothered about him, in fact they ignored him when he joined the prancing circle.

Six times he ran round the fire, bending low and stretching up, and on the seventh circuit, as if by accident, he moved in so close that his headdress caught alight.

At once the dancers rushed at Rabbit
to put out the flames. But he dodged this
way and that, and Rabbit was very good at
dodging. He was nearly at the gate of the
stockade when one of the dancers made a
great grab and seized his ears.

Ay, ay, ay, it was agony. But Rabbit pulled
and wriggled away. He escaped, though his
ears had been stretched to three times their
normal length.

Outside the stockade he fled, tumbling
down the mountainside. Now both his
headdress and his jacket were on fire,
singeing his back. One of the Sky People
threw a tomahawk at him. It struck his nose,
splitting it down the middle. But still he
ran on.

Now the whole tribe came thundering after
him. The leaders began to overtake him. Fear
and burning pain made Rabbit desperate.
Maybe, he thought, I can run more swiftly on
four legs than two – perhaps twice as fast.

So down on all fours he went and shot

away. But not before one of the pursuers seized hold of his splendid curly tail. With a great jerk, Rabbit got away again – leaving most of it behind. In the end, the Sky People gave up the chase.

At last he reached the lands of the Earth People, bringing fire. It was passed from one village to another. They were saved.

Now, for a little while, everyone said Rabbit was a hero, though they also thought he was rather funny. He had extra-long ears, and a very short tail, a split nose and a light brown patch down his back, where the fire had burnt him. And when he was alarmed he ran on all fours. In fact, he began to look like just another furry animal, though he could go on two legs if he needed.

And he needed it very much, because during the winter months when hunting was difficult, some of the bigger creatures, like Wolf, began to cast around for game. Wolf thought to himself, Now Rabbit should be easy to catch. He doesn't seem to know what day of the week it is.

Well, it wasn't long before Rabbit guessed that Wolf was on his trail. So, what did he do?

He would walk upright for a while, then run like fury on all fours, then back on two legs.

Wolf, hard on his track, would stop and say, "That's funny, I could have sworn that was a Rabbit footprint, but now it seems I'm following a man. I'd better be careful."

One day, on the trail of Rabbit, Wolf came to a clearing in the forest, where an old man was standing.

"Hello, Wolf," called the old man cheerfully, "what are you doing in this neck of the woods?"

"Tell me, old man," said Wolf, eyeing him very keenly "have you seen Rabbit round here?"

"Rabbit?" came the reply. "Not likely. He vanished like a puff of smoke when you came along."

Wolf was baffled. He looked carefully at

the friendly old chap.

"Tell me, why are your ears so long, grandad?"

"That? Just a trick of the light. My hair stands up at the back. I can't do a thing with it."

"Your nose is a bit strange, too."

"Oh, that, it runs in the family."

"But it's split, like a rabbit's."

"I see what you mean. That's where I bumped into a rock last week."

Now the Wolf looked down suspiciously.

"Your toes are yellow, just like a rabbit's."

"Oh, that. A bad habit, smoking. I hold the pipe in my toes when my hands are full."

Wolf decided he wasn't going to get any sense out of the old fellow, so he said goodbye and left him alone. But when he was a little distance away he looked back and saw the "old man" dashing away in the other direction, on all fours.

Grinding his teeth, Wolf decided he must now use cunning. So, it happened one day, that as Rabbit tracked through the woods, he met Wolf in great distress. His foot seemed to be trapped under a boulder.

"Rabbit, old friend," he groaned. "Help me out and you and I will be pals for ever."

Rabbit, without thinking, lifted the boulder. Set free, Wolf grabbed him. "Now I've got you," he snarled.

"That was a rotten trick," cried Rabbit.

"Hah. Didn't you trick me? Come on, off to my den with you," growled Wolf in triumph.

But on the way, they met Fox, and Rabbit appealed to him. "Is it fair Wolf should eat me when I helped him?"

"Ah," said sly Fox. "I can't judge the case till I see how things were from the start."

Back they went to the boulder. Wolf lay down and Rabbit put it back on his leg.

"Now then, Rabbit, look smart," said Fox and the two raced away, leaving Wolf howling with rage.

"How can I thank you?" Rabbit asked Fox

and Fox answered, "Don't bother. I'm planning to eat you myself."

At this, Rabbit gave a great leap in the air, went down on all fours and shot away, his short tail bobbing behind him, his long ears laid straight along his back.

And that is how rabbits have been ever since. If you see someone on two legs who says he's a rabbit, or someone on four legs who says he's a man, don't you believe him.

Who's a Clever Boy, Then?

Who's a
Clever Boy, Then?

....

Jack was a bold lad with curly hair and bright
eyes and quick on his feet. But the quickest
part of him was his tongue. His long-suffering
mother told him, "One of these days you'll
talk yourself into a lot of trouble."

He laughed, as he always did. "Don't you
worry, Ma. I'll talk my way out again."

And he did. Before he was eighteen, he'd
talked himself right out of the family home.
Here's how it happened. He was on his way
down the lane one day when an old cottage
woman asked him, "Now then, Jack, where's
your dad?"

"Oh, him," answered Jack. "He's enjoying
our misfortune."

"Whatever does that mean, Jack?"

"Well, the old mare died."

"That's bad."

"So it is. But he's got the money to buy a new one."

"Oh, that's all right then."

"No, it's not. He's already spent it all."

"Get off with you, Jack. Where's your mother?"

"Oh, she's setting a dough for last month's bread."

"How can she do that?"

"Nothing easier. Last month we hadn't a loaf in the house, so Ma borrowed some. Now she's baking bread to pay the neighbours back."

The old woman laughed till the tears came. "You're a clever lad, you are. Watch you don't come to a bad end."

"Everybody comes to a bad end, grannie."

"How d'you make that out, Jack?"

"'Cause none of us wants to go, do we?"

The dame was so tickled with Jack's answers she took him to her hive and gave him a big jar of honey. Jack took it home and put it on the shelf in the kitchen. Then he told his mother, "That's going to make my fortune, see."

"Oh yes, and pigs might fly," said she.

"Now you listen, Ma," said Jack strutting round the kitchen table. "I'm going to sell that for sixpence and buy six eggs. When they hatch out, they'll all be cock chicks, so I'll swap three for hens. In no time at all I'll have twelve dozen eggs. Them I shall sell at market and buy a plot of land. Soon I'll have crops and cattle and before you know it, I'll be a fine gent and marry Milord's daughter."

His mother stared at him with mouth wide open. "And where will your poor mother and father be then, Jack?"

"Ma," said Jack, "I shall hardly know where I am myself, so how can I say?"

"Why, you young rogue," snapped his mother and gave her son such a shove he banged into the kitchen wall. Down came the jar from the shelf and his fame and fortune broke over his head and ran straight down his neck.

Jack decided to try his luck away from the

family home. But there weren't many jobs around that would pay enough for him to wed Milord's daughter.

So, he took a short cut and joined a band of robbers hiding in the woods. At first they didn't want to have him. "For all we know, you may be useless," said the robber chief.

"Well, I'll show you," said Jack.

Next day he lay in wait by the high road. First he took off his left shoe and put it on the road. Along came a farmer leading a fat ox to market. He saw the shoe but left it lying. What was the good of one shoe?

But Jack nipped smartly forward by a short cut and put his right shoe on the road ahead. That was more like it, thought the farmer when he came along – I can use a pair of shoes. So he tied the ox to a tree and went back for the left shoe while Jack quietly untied the ox and led it away.

The very next day Jack played the same trick on another farmer and came back to the hideout with a couple of sheep. The robbers were delighted. Without more ado, they sacked their leader and put Jack in his place.

He returned the compliment by giving them all the day off. And while they were off he helped himself to the gold they had hidden away. Then he took the ox and the sheep back to their owners and went off into town to buy himself a brand-new outfit and a feather for his cap.

Next Sunday he turned up in church like a conquering hero. The whole district knew of his exploits. The priest didn't think much of them, though, and preached a great sermon about rogues in fine feathers. But this only made all the congregation turn round and look at Jack, including Milord and his lovely daughter Alice, who liked what she saw.

This went on three Sundays in a row. The priest got madder and madder, but Jack and Alice looked at each other all the way through the service. So afterwards, bold as brass, Jack went up to Milord and, sweeping off his fine hat with its long feather, asked for Alice's hand in marriage.

Milord didn't get angry. He didn't look down his nose at Jack. He just laughed. "You *look* a fine fellow. You think you're a fine fellow. But are you as smart as you think? I don't want a windbag for a son-in-law."

"You just try me, Milord."

"Very well then," said Milord, who loved a wager. "I'll bet you cannot steal the goose off the roasting spit in the Hall kitchen."

"Done," said Jack.

Next day he went out in the field and caught two hares. Then he put on a dirty old cloak like a beggar and went to the kitchen door at the Hall. No one paid him the slightest heed.

That is until he let the hares go. There was pandemonium as they raced round and round the kitchen. Dogs, scullions, kitchen maid, cook all chased after them, while Jack walked away with the roast, as cool as a cucumber.

How Milord laughed. But he still shook his head. "That was easy."

Jack gritted his teeth. "Try me again," he challenged.

"Very well. Tonight take my six racing horses out of my stables."

"No sooner said than done," answered Jack.

But Milord didn't intend it to be easy. He ordered six grooms to sit on the backs of the horses and not stir all night. Off he went to bed, laughing.

At midnight, the stable door opened and in shuffled a shivering old woman in rags. "Can I come in out of the cold, boys?" she wheedled.

The grooms paid her no heed until they saw her swigging from what looked like a brandy bottle. They were sleepy and their toes were dropping off with cold, so when the old beldame pulled another bottle out of her cloak and offered it round, they each had a good long pull. Before you could say Jack

Robinson, they were fast asleep and falling off the backs of their horses while Jack was leading the whole string away, sweet as kiss your hand.

Now Milord had to admit Jack had won. And since Alice had already made up her mind, he gave his consent and the two were to be wed that next month.

But the priest point blank refused to do the honours. "You are wrong, Milord," he said pompously, "to be taken in by such simple tricks. No person of intellect would be deceived by this rogue."

"Ho ho," mumured Milord, "you think so, eh?" And he winked to Jack, who took the hint.

At midnight the church bell began to toll mournfully. The sexton looked inside the church, then ran for the priest. "The Angel of Death's by the altar, master," he said.

The priest ran into the nave. "What's this, what's this?" he blustered. Then he fell on his knees as a great figure in white rose up before him in the shadows.

"Your time has come to be judged!" called a mighty rolling voice.

"Will I be saved?" quavered the priest.

"Into my soul hamper," commanded the figure in white. The priest obeyed, the lid was slammed shut and the basket was hauled bumping and slamming round the churchyard until the minister was out of his wits with fear.

After that the priest had a lot less to say for himself and when next month came around, Alice and Jack were wed with all the trimmings before the whole town.

And there in Milord's family pew sat Jack's father and mother. His mother, decked out in a fine new dress and hat, turned to the people behind her with great condescension.

"There!" she said, "Didn't I tell you our boy would make his fortune?"

And nobody could contradict her.

Idle Jack

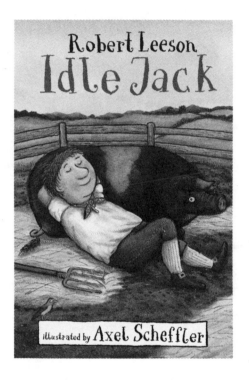

Jack Patch is a very lazy boy,
who somehow manages to come
out on top in every situation!

Smart Girls

Shortlisted for the Guardian Children's
Book Prize, these folk tales are about
smart heroines around the world.

Smart Girls Forever

The feisty heroines of these six folk tales

all share one important quality:

they are extremely SMART!

Robert Leeson (1928–2013) wrote many books for children, including *Smart Girls* (shortlisted for the Guardian Fiction Prize), *Smart Girls Forever*, *Idle Jack* and *Lucky Lad*. In 1985 he received the Eleanor Farjeon Award for his services to children's literature.

Axel Scheffler is an award-winning, internationally acclaimed illustrator of some of the most well-loved children's books, most famously *The Gruffalo*, written by Julia Donaldson. His books have been published in many languages and his work has been exhibited all around the world.